PUFFIN BOOKS

THE BIRD WITH GOLDEN WINGS

Sudha Murty was born in 1950 in Shiggaon in north Karnataka. She did her MTech in computer science, and is now the chairperson of the Infosys Foundation. A prolific writer in English and Kannada, she has written novels, technical books, travelogues, collections of short stories and non-fictional pieces, and four books for children. Her books have been translated into all the major Indian languages. Sudha Murty was the recipient of the R.K. Narayan Award for Literature and the Padma Shri in 2006, and the Attimabbe Award from the government of Karnataka for excellence in Kannada literature in 2011.

D1150408

Read More in Puffin by Sudha Murty

SUDHA MURTY

THE BIRD WITH GOLDEN WINGS

STORIES OF WIT AND MAGIC

Illustrations by Ajanta Guhathakurta

PUFFIN BOOKS

An imprint of Penguin Random House

PUFFIN BOOKS

USA | Canada | UK | Ireland | Australia
New Zealand | India | South Africa | China

Puffin Books is part of the Penguin Random House group of companies
whose addresses can be found at global.penguinrandomhouse.com

Published by Penguin Random House India Pvt. Ltd
4th Floor, Capital Tower 1, MG Road,
Gurugram 122 002, Haryana, India

Penguin
Random House
India

First published in Puffin by Penguin Books India 2009
This edition published 2016

Text copyright © Sudha Murty 2009
Illustrations copyright © Ajanta Guhathakurta 2009

All rights reserved

47 46

ISBN 9780143334255

Typeset in Sabon MT by Manipal Digital Systems, Manipal
Printed at Thomson Press India Ltd, New Delhi

www.penguin.co.in

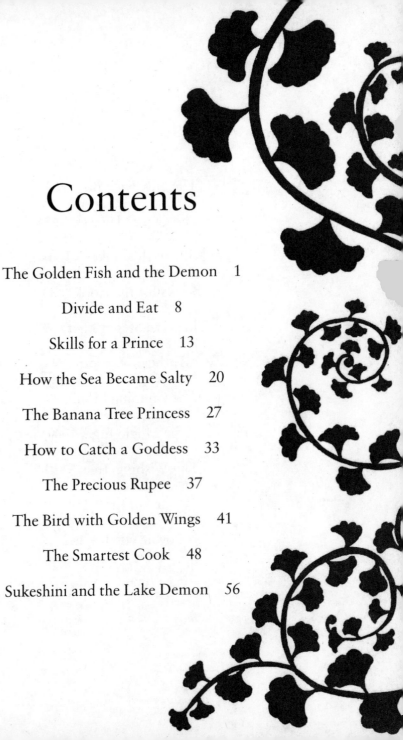

Contents

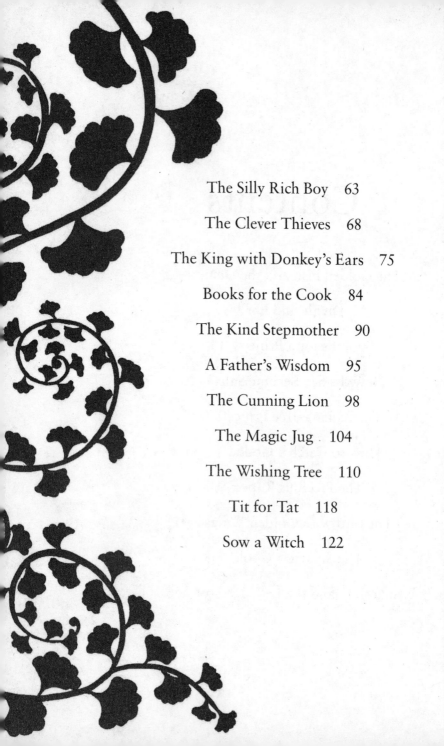

The Golden Fish and the Demon

Suraj was a fisherman. He lived with his wife Lakshmi in a little village by the sea. Suraj would sail his boat into the sea every day to catch fish. He would come back with his small net full of fish, enough to earn him a little money. The couple was poor and did not have any children. While Suraj was a nice, kind man, Lakshmi always felt she knew best and loved telling Suraj what to do in a loud voice. For the sake of some peace and quiet, Suraj did exactly as his wife told him.

One morning, Lakshmi strode up to where Suraj was sitting and eating his breakfast before leaving to catch fish and shouted, 'There is no firewood in the house. How will I cook? You must get some wood from the market when you return home this evening.'

Suraj nodded quietly, picked up his net and set off. He sat in his boat for a long time that day, his net trailing in the water, but could not trap a single fish. At sunset, Suraj decided to give up and head home. Worried about the scolding he would get from his wife, Suraj slowly pulled his net from the water. To his surprise, it felt heavy. When he pulled it out of the water, he was astonished to see a tiny golden-coloured fish trapped in the net. Just as he was about to throw the fish into the bucket kept next to him, it spoke in a human voice.

'Please don't take me. Leave me in the sea. I will give you whatever you want.'

Suraj was scared. Such a thing had never happened to him in all the years he had gone fishing. But the fish did look quite sad, and he felt bad for it. Who would want to buy such a small fish anyway, he thought, and he threw it back into the water. As it landed with a splash, the fish said in a loud voice, 'Thank you for saving me. Tell me what you want and I shall fulfil your wish.'

In a flash Suraj remembered his wife's command to bring home some firewood. He shouted, 'My wife wants firewood to use in our kitchen. Can you please give me some?'

The fish replied, 'Go home. Your wish will be fulfilled.'

Suraj went home, feeling a little nervous. What if the fish did not keep its promise? Lakshmi would be furious, and would not believe his story either! But as he neared his home, he saw the entire courtyard was filled with firewood. He clapped his hands in glee and rushed to his wife. He told her all about the fish. But Lakshmi was not happy at all! Suraj had been granted a wish and all he had asked for was firewood! 'You silly fish-head!' she screamed. 'Go back right now and ask the fish to give us some food as well. Do you think we can fill our stomachs with firewood?'

Suraj trudged back to the seashore and called out to his little fish friend. There was a flash of light in the dark waters and the fish came swimming up, right in front of him. Suraj joined his palms and said very politely, 'O little golden fish, my wife is not satisfied with just firewood. She has told me to ask you for some food as well.'

The fish leaped, did a little twirl in the air and said, 'So be it.' Then it was gone in the twinkling of an eye.

Suraj hurried back home and, sure enough, his house was full of sacks of foodgrain, enough to last them for many months. Lakshmi, too, looked happy and for a few days there was peace in the house.

Then one day Lakshmi had to go visit her friend in the next village. As she took out her two good saris from the cupboard, she complained loudly, 'What can we do with only grains? How can they make us look good? Just see this tattered old sari I am wearing. My friend will laugh when she sees me wearing it. Go and ask the fish for some grand clothes for us.'

Suraj knew he could not argue with his wife, so he walked to the sea and called out to the golden fish. Again, the fish appeared as soon as Suraj called, and when he asked for new clothes, it did a twirl in the air and granted the wish. For a few days, Lakshmi was happy and had a wonderful time at her friend's house showing off her shiny new saris.

Then she became gloomy again. 'What is the use of food, clothing and wood? We require a better house. Go and ask your fish for it,' she told her husband.

Suraj did as she asked, and the fish granted him this wish as well.

After some time, Lakshmi thought of another demand. 'Ask the fish to give us plenty of gold so that we need not ask for anything again.'

This time, too, her wish was fulfilled. Suraj was also happy. He would not have to come to the sea any more and beg the fish for different things. But Lakshmi could not rest. Now that they had a huge house and pots of gold, she became scared that thieves would come and steal everything.

'Do you have any sense or not?' she shouted at her husband. 'What if we are attacked by robbers at night? We will lose all this hard-won wealth. Go and tell your fish to do something so that no one ever dares come near us, or tries to steal from us.'

Poor Suraj went again to the seashore and called out to the fish. As had happened earlier, when the fish appeared, Suraj told the fish what he wanted in exactly the words his wife had used. This time, too, the fish leaped up and dived back into the water after granting the wish.

Slowly, Suraj walked home, wondering what would happen to them. As he neared his house, he noticed a strange, hairy, demon-like creature standing near the door. It was big, with muscular arms, two horns on its head, long nails on its fingers, and huge teeth. When it saw him, it came rushing up and, to his horror, Suraj realized Lakshmi had been transformed into a fearful demon! Now no one would ever dare to come near them or try to steal their gold.

Lakshmi stood in front of him and burst into tears. 'Your fish has played a trick on us! It has made me look like this so that no one will want to be near me. Hurry! Don't just stand there, go and tell him to turn me back into the way I was!'

Suraj ran all the way to the sea. There, he called and called, requesting his little golden fish friend to come out. But it did not appear. No one saw the fish or Suraj ever again. And greedy Lakshmi remained a demon till the day she died—a rich, old woman but with no friends.

Divide and Eat

Once upon a time, there were two brothers. Though they were twins, they were as different from each other as chalk and cheese. While Ramesh was well built, cheerful and always ready to help people in need, Suresh was thin, quiet and a miser. The brothers did not get along well with each other and spent all their time quarrelling, much to their mother's annoyance.

When they were twenty years old, they decided to leave their village and go to the big city to make a living. On their way to the city, they had to cross a forest. The two walked through the forest, arguing as usual. It was a hot day, and when they reached a huge banyan tree, standing under its soothing shade, they finally agreed on something—that they were ravenously hungry! Quickly, they opened their bags and took out the lunch boxes their mother had packed for them. Knowing well they would argue bitterly if they had to share their lunch, their mother had packed two boxes.

There were other travellers, too, who had stopped to eat their food under the shade of the tree, and some

were taking a restful nap before carrying on.
The brothers washed their hands in a nearby
stream and opened their boxes. To their
surprise, they saw that while Ramesh
had been given three parathas, there
were only two in Suresh's tiffin box.
Perhaps their mother thought Ramesh, with
his hearty appetite, would need to eat more.
But Suresh was very upset. So what if he
couldn't eat more than two parathas, how
dare Mother give him less, he fumed.

As they were about to start eating, a traveller came up to them and said, 'Brothers, I am sorry to interrupt your meal, but I have lost my way. I am very hungry. I have money in my pocket, but where can I buy food in this forest? If you share your food with me, I will pay you for it.' Suresh readily agreed, always happy to earn some money. Ramesh nodded too, but because he felt sorry for the stranger and wanted to help him.

The three settled down and divided up all the parathas amongst themselves. They ate till they were full. The traveller was delighted. Even the simplest of meals can taste like a king's banquet when you are famished! When they had finished, they washed up. The traveller placed five silver coins in front of them and said, 'You shared your food with me when I was about to faint with hunger. May god bless you. I will take your leave now.'

Ramesh took three of the five coins and gave the remaining two to his brother. Suresh was very angry! 'We shared our food equally with the man, so I should get half of whatever he gave us. You should give me another half-coin.'

Ramesh smiled and said, 'I shared three parathas, while you shared two. So I should get three coins and you should get two. But if you are unhappy with this division, I don't mind giving you a half-coin from my share. I don't have any change at the moment, though. When we reach the city, I'll give you your remaining share.'

But Suresh was in no mood to wait. 'I want my half-coin right now!' he demanded. Helplessly, Ramesh went to another traveller who was dozing under the tree and perhaps listening to their argument. When Ramesh asked him for change, the man removed the scarf with which he had covered his face and, smiling, said, 'I have heard everything. You cannot get three coins. If you want, I can work out exactly how much each one of you should get.'

Ramesh and Suresh agreed that they would share the coins exactly as per the man's instructions. The man sat up straight, crossed his legs, closed his eyes and told them, 'Listen to me carefully. The two of you together had five parathas. When the stranger joined you, there were three of you. Now if you divide each paratha into three pieces, that makes fifteen pieces in all. If fifteen pieces have to be eaten equally by three people, each one will get five pieces. Ramesh, from your three parathas you had nine pieces, of which you ate five and gave the stranger four. Suresh, from your two parathas, you had six pieces. Of these six, you ate five pieces and gave one to the stranger. So the man got four pieces from Ramesh and one from you. To make a fair division of the five coins he gave, Ramesh should get four coins and Suresh one.'

Suresh was very upset—his share was even lesser now! But he had to agree with this clever bit of maths.

Skills for a Prince

Amritsena, a young prince, was very popular with his subjects. Everyone praised his sense of fairness. He also loved to play pranks and made the courtiers laugh. He often disguised himself and roamed the streets of the capital city, listening to what the people were saying, and learnt about the problems of the common man this way.

During one such tour, he came across three young men on the outskirts of the city. From their attire they appeared to be strangers. They were huddled together, talking to each other.

Amritsena walked up to them and said, 'You look new to this city. Can I help you?'

One of the men replied, 'We are students of Sage Kashyapa and have recently finished our studies. We are looking for work where we can put our special skills to use.'

At once, Amritsena's ears pricked up. 'And what are these special skills? I work in the king's court and I may be able to help you find a job there.'

One of the young men said, 'Just by tapping my feet, I can make out what is below the ground.'

The second one said, 'I can always tell which direction one may find hidden treasure in.'

The third said, 'Once I have seen a person, I can recognize him anywhere, even if he is in disguise.'

Amritsena heard them out, thought for a minute and said, 'I am also a man with a special quality.'

'What is that?' they asked.

'If anyone is in difficulty, I can always find a solution and rescue the person.'

'From where did you get this gift? Who taught you?'

'I have always had this gift, from when I was a child,' replied Amritsena with a smile. Then he said, 'Why don't you show me a sample of your special skills as we walk to the city? I can then tell the king about you.'

The four men began walking. After some time, one stopped and said, 'Below us lies a tunnel.'

They started digging and, sure enough, they found a tunnel. They began to walk through the tunnel, which led them into the palace.

Now the second man stopped suddenly and said, 'Just around the corner there is a secret treasury.'

Amritsena, who knew this to be true, was amazed. He smiled secretly to himself and said, 'You three wait here. If the guards see you they will mistake you for thieves. Let me go and check.' Then he walked quickly ahead, turned a corner where he stripped off his disguise, and presented himself before the guards.

'There are three men in the tunnel plotting to loot the treasury,' he told them. 'Go and arrest them immediately. They should be produced in court first thing tomorrow morning.' Saying this, he walked away to his room and went to bed.

The next morning, the three men were presented in the king's court. Seeing Amritsena on the throne, the third man realized he was the same man who had got them arrested. He whispered this to his friends. Now they were scared that the prince would punish them for having entered the royal treasury just to show off.

'How did you find the way into the secret tunnel?' thundered the king, Amritsena's father.

'We . . . we j-just . . .' stammered the men, shaking in fear.

Amritsena watched them, trying not to laugh. Then he stepped in and whispered in his father's ear, 'They are not thieves. I met them last night just outside the city. They are learned men with wonderful gifts. I only wanted to test them to see if they were telling the truth. We should keep them in our kingdom as their talents will help us in many ways.'

The king nodded and said, 'On the request of the prince I release you. You will work for me from now on, and use your gifts for the betterment of this kingdom.'

The three men sighed with relief. Amritsena had rescued them—just as he had said he could!

How the Sea Became Salty

 A long, long time ago, seawater was sweet and drinkable. How it became salty is a remarkable story.

Sridhar was an orphan. He stayed with his brother Keshav and his sister-in-law Leela. While Keshav was quiet and kind, Leela was mean and selfish. She resented Sridhar staying with them. She would not give him enough to eat, made him work very hard and found many ways to trouble him. Keshav could never gather the courage to stop his wife from treating his brother so badly.

One day, Leela told Sridhar to get firewood. Obediently he went to the nearby forest with his axe and chopped some wood. Then he bundled the sticks and returned, just as it was getting dark. On seeing him, Leela shouted, 'Look how late you are! What took you so long? Is this any time to come home? When will I light the kitchen fire, and when will I cook?' Then looking carefully, she asked, 'Where is the axe?

If you have left it in the forest, you have to return right now and get it. I will not allow you to enter the house without it.'

Poor Sridhar had to walk back into the forest in the dark. The shadows were dense and there was no moonlight to help him either. He searched everywhere but could not find the axe. Without realizing it, he wandered deeper and deeper into the forest as he searched. Suddenly, storm clouds gathered and rain started pouring down. Sridhar spotted a flicker of light in the distance and ran towards it. The light was coming from a fire, which had been lit inside a small cave. Sridhar dashed in and, to his surprise, saw his axe lying in the cave next to some firewood. Then, as he looked carefully, some dwarves emerged from the shadows. Without taking any notice of him, they gathered around the fire and, holding hands, began to dance.

As Sridhar stood and watched them in amazement, an old dwarf with a long white beard came up to him and said, 'Come and join our dance.' But Sridhar was wonderstruck and did not know what to do. He noticed that the fire was starting to burn out, so he chopped the firewood into smaller pieces and fed the fire. The night passed—with the dwarves dancing and Sridhar

feeding the fire with fresh wood when it looked like it was dying.

The dwarves were very happy. When dawn broke and their celebrations ended, one of them came up to Sridhar and said, 'You helped us so much last night. We have a gift for you.

Here is a fan. Whenever you desire something, just wave the fan gently and ask for it. When you've got enough, whisper "Enough, enough, enough", and it will stop producing the objects.' Saying this, he handed Sridhar what looked like an ordinary fan. Then the group of dwarves swiftly melted into the forest.

Sridhar could not believe his luck! Just to try out the fan, he waved it in the air and said, 'Get me a hot meal.' As soon as he said this, dishes started falling from the sky, each filled with all kinds of delicious food. Sridhar whispered hurriedly, 'Enough, enough, enough,' and the dishes stopped appearing. Sridhar sat down and ate a hearty meal, his first in many years. Then he lay down in the shade of a large tree and pondered what he should do next. He decided not to go back to his brother's house. Instead, he went to a beautiful town near the sea and there, he built a house, made money and never wanted for anything, thanks to the magic fan.

When Keshav and Leela heard that Sridhar was now living in a town near the sea and was very prosperous, they became jealous. They quickly packed their bags and went to meet him. Sridhar, who had always been very fond of his brother, greeted them politely and asked them to spend as much time as they wanted in his house. Keshav and Leela were wonderstruck seeing the riches Sridhar had acquired. Leela told her husband that night, 'How is it that your stupid brother has become so rich and we are still trying to make ends meet in the village? You must ask him his secret tomorrow.'

The next day, when Keshav questioned him, Sridhar told him, 'Oh, I just got lucky. I was presented with a magic fan. When I wave it and ask for what I want, the fan produces it out of thin air. When I have enough . . .' Keshav did not have the patience to hear any more. 'That's nice,' he said. 'May god bless you.' Then he ran to tell Leela the story, whose greedy eyes glittered when she heard it. She *had* to get her hands on that fan!

That night, when everyone was asleep, she made Keshav creep into the room where the fan was kept and steal it. Then the two of them ran out of the house, clutching the fan and bags filled with valuables stolen from Sridhar's house. They ran till they reached the harbour. A big ship was just about to leave.

Leela said, 'Why don't we leave this country once and for all? With this fan, we can make a good life for ourselves in any place.' As usual, Keshav agreed, and the two boarded the ship. Seeing them, the captain asked, 'Are you two new around here? Who are you?'

Quickly, Leela answered, 'My husband is a salt merchant. We are going to other countries to try and sell salt there. Our bags contain only salt.'

Next day, at lunch time, the cook of the ship came and complained to the captain, 'My new helper boy left

the sack of salt at the harbour. We are without any salt in the kitchen. How will I serve food to the passengers?'

The captain immediately remembered the salt merchant on his ship. 'Don't worry,' he told the cook, 'I'll get some salt for you.' Then he went to Keshav and said, 'If you don't mind, can we buy one sack of salt from you for the ship's kitchen?'

Keshav had to say yes. He and Leela went to a corner of the ship and waved the fan. 'Give us salt,' they said. Immediately, sacks full of salt started falling from the sky. But the couple did not know how to stop the magic fan. 'Stop!' they yelled. Still the sacks kept falling. 'Cease! Halt! Discontinue!' they shouted. But they never got the right words—enough, enough, enough.

Many sacks of salt fell from the sky. The ship overturned and sank. The salt spilled into the sea. It rained salt sacks for many, many days, till the dwarves heard about it and made the fan stop with their magic. But by then the sea was full of salt which had dissolved in the water. And the sea remained salty for ever after.

The Banana Tree
Princess

 There lived a prince who was the only child of his parents, and they doted on him. But like all princes in ancient times, he was sent away to a school in the forest to study and train to be a warrior. When he returned home, he had grown into a handsome and smart young man. The king and queen were delighted to have him back in the palace and were now keen that he choose a princess and marry her. They made him meet many smart girls, but the prince did not choose any of them. He wanted to find the prettiest, most quick-witted girl in the whole country.

The prince loved gardening and tended the royal gardens himself. He planted trees and flowers from all over the world there. As a result, the garden was full of wonderful, exotic plants and bushes.

The prince's special pride and joy was a unique mango tree, which produced fruit all-year round. The mangoes were golden in colour and tasted as sweet as sugar. There was no other mango tree like that anywhere in the country. The prince was very proud of his tree. He gathered the fruit and gifted them only to a select few people, who coveted this remarkable gift.

One day, as he was inspecting his garden, he looked at the mango tree and, to his shock, realized that some fruits were missing. Immediately he summoned the guards and told them to be on full alert. The sentries positioned themselves around the tree. Yet, the next morning when the prince arrived, he saw some more fruits had been stolen. This time, the prince got the wall around the garden raised and lined with spikes. But the mangoes were missing yet again the next day.

The prince decided to stay awake and guard the tree himself. He hid behind a bush to keep watch. In the middle of the night, a mild and attractive perfume wafted through the garden. In no time, the prince fell asleep. When he got up in the morning, as usual, the mangoes were missing.

He realized that the perfume put everyone to sleep. So he decided that he would cover his nose with a scarf and not breathe in the scent as he kept watch the next night.

In the darkest hour of the night, the prince, from his hiding place, saw an amazing sight. Near the mango tree was an ordinary banana tree. The most beautiful girl

the prince had
ever seen emerged
from the banana tree. In
her hands, she held a golden pot.
She filled the pot with some mangoes.
Then she disappeared into the banana tree. All
this while, the prince just sat behind the bush, unable to
believe what he was seeing.

The next day the prince decided to catch the girl.
As soon as she came out of the banana tree, he cut the
tree. When the maiden finished plucking the mangoes
and turned to make her way into the banana tree, to her
shock, she found the tree gone and the way barred by
an angry prince.

The prince said to her, 'Why have you been stealing
from my garden? You must make amends for this.
You are the most beautiful woman I have ever laid my
eyes on. Marry me, and I will give you as many mangoes
as you want.'

The woman looked down and said, 'I come from
another world, from beyond the banana tree. I know I
should not have stolen the mangoes. But I tasted them
once, and had to keep coming back to take more. If
you want, I will marry you. But you must fulfil one
condition.'

The prince asked what her condition was. She said, 'I will always keep this pot with me. You must never, ever open it. The day you open it, I will return to my own world. If you agree to this, we can marry.'

The prince agreed immediately, and without giving it further thought, got married. The prince loved his wife dearly, and she too got used to her new life in the palace. They were very happy together.

One day, when she was away, the prince happened to go to her chambers. Walking around, his eyes fell on the golden pot which she had carried in her hands when they first met. He remembered the

strange condition she had set before agreeing to marry him. 'But now she loves me,' he thought to himself. 'If I open the pot, she will surely not leave me! I have to open it and see what's inside.'

With these thoughts in his mind, the prince whipped off the cover of the pot and peered inside. There was nothing there! The prince burst into laughter. 'Oh, it was only a joke! It is an empty pot, and surely she will not leave me for an empty pot!'

His wife had entered the room and was standing behind him. She had seen and heard everything. Now she came up to him and said, 'To you the pot may look empty, but when you promised never to open it, it began to contain trust, as well as my dreams of leading a happy life with you. Trust is what makes any relationship successful. By breaking your promise, you have destroyed the faith that kept us together. And without trust and dreams, life has no meaning. I cannot live with you any more. I have to leave you now.'

And in the blink of an eye, the golden pot and the maiden disappeared, leaving the prince sad and alone.

How to Catch a Goddess

Rohini was a smart woman, married to a rich merchant. For many years they lived happily. Then, the merchant suffered losses in his business, and they had to give up the large mansion in which they stayed. They had to move to a small hut at the edge of the city. The hut was surrounded by trees and tall grass.

Rohini did not have any servants now. She had to do all the housework herself. She cooked and cleaned and washed. One day, as she was putting the washed clothes out to dry, she spotted something glittering in the tall grass. She bent down and looked closely. It was a gorgeous diamond necklace! 'Such a necklace is fit only for a queen. It must have been stolen from the palace. Perhaps a thief dropped it here as he was escaping, or maybe a bird carried it away in its beak.' While she was holding the necklace and wondering what to do, the town crier passed by.

'Queen Kamala lost her diamond necklace when she was taking a bath. She had kept her necklace near the pond in her garden and a bird took it. If anybody finds the necklace it should be returned to the queen. She has promised a handsome reward in return.'

Rohini had guessed right. She went straight to the palace, where she presented the queen with the necklace. Queen Kamala was delighted. 'This is my most favourite ornament,' she said. 'You deserve a gift. Tell me, what is it that you want?'

But Rohini was silent. The queen coaxed her, 'Do not be afraid. I cannot let you go empty-handed. Do you want gold? A bigger house? Nice clothes?'

Finally, Rohini spoke up. 'I do not want any of these, Your Majesty.'

'Then what is it that you wish for?'

'I have a request. On this Diwali night no one must light any lamps in the kingdom. Not even you. The entire city must be in darkness, except for my house, where I shall light candles.'

The queen was amazed by this strange request. Everyone lit diyas in their house on Diwali! But she had to keep her word, so she agreed.

Soon it was Diwali. Rohini spent the whole day cleaning her hut and its surroundings. That night, all around her hut, she lit as many candles as she could find. And as per the queen's orders, no other house lit candles—the entire city was in darkness. Rohini sat at her doorstep, with materials for worship ready at her side.

Lakshmi, the goddess of wealth, comes to earth every Diwali night. That night, when she descended on the city, she was astonished to find it in darkness. 'How strange!' she thought. 'On Diwali night everyone lights lamps to welcome me. But I see not a single light, except for some candles in that hut.' So Lakshmi made her way to Rohini's house.

Looking at Lakshmi standing before her, with her dazzling beauty and ornaments, Rohini knew who she was. She knelt down and worshipped the goddess with a lot of devotion. Then, as Lakshmi, happy with the welcome, was about to step into her house, Rohini stopped her. Lakshmi looked at her in amazement. Whoever stops Goddess Lakshmi from entering?

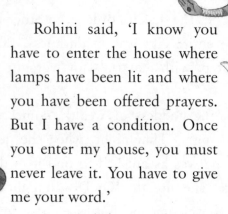

Rohini said, 'I know you have to enter the house where lamps have been lit and where you have been offered prayers. But I have a condition. Once you enter my house, you must never leave it. You have to give me your word.'

Now Lakshmi understood everything. She smiled and nodded. 'You are a brave and clever person, Rohini,' she said. 'I will be happy to stay in your house.' Saying this, the goddess entered Rohini's house, never to leave it again. And thus, Rohini and her husband were able to get back all their lost wealth and were never poor again.

The Precious Rupee

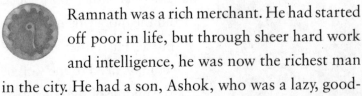 Ramnath was a rich merchant. He had started off poor in life, but through sheer hard work and intelligence, he was now the richest man in the city. He had a son, Ashok, who was a lazy, good-for-nothing boy. While everyone his age was studying and then trying to earn a living, Ashok was happy to live off his father's wealth. He had never done a day's work in his life.

Ashok decided he wanted his own business, so he went to his father and said, 'I need some money to start a business of my own.' Ramnath, who was always worried about his son's attitude to work, said, 'To run a successful business you don't need only money. You also need to work hard. Are you willing to put in that effort?' But Ashok was not ready to listen to any advice. He only wanted the money. Ramnath thought for a while and said, 'Very well, I will lend you the money, but on one condition. You must give me one rupee every day until I tell you to stop.' Ashok argued, 'What if you never tell me to stop?' 'I will ask you to stop, and soon,' his father assured him with a smile.

It seemed a strange but easy request to fulfil, so Ashok agreed. The next day, he gave his father one rupee from the money he had in his purse. His father took the coin, walked to the well in the middle of the courtyard and threw it into the well. Ashok was shocked. Over the next few months, Ashok gave all the money he had to his father, who, in turn, threw the coins into the well.

Then Ashok asked his mother to give him money. His mother helped him for a few days, then she too ran out of money, and said, 'Why should I give you any money if it's going to end up at the bottom of the well?' She stopped giving him money.

Ashok then went to his sister and asked for money. She helped him for a few days, but later she protested too, 'Why should I give my money to have it thrown into the well?'

He asked many relatives. All of them helped only for a few days. Finally, Ashok was forced to run his business to earn money. But no one wanted to do business with him as they knew he was lazy and spoilt.

Ashok now had to work for a living, and the only work he could get was that of a farm labourer. He had never lifted a finger in his life, so he found a day's work of digging fields and feeding cows back-breaking. At the end of the day he earned a meagre five rupees. From this he had to give a rupee to his father. Ramnath pretended not to notice the pain his son was in and taking the coin given to him, flung it into the well.

The next day Ashok had to walk even further for work. Again he worked hard all day in the fierce sun to earn a small sum of money. His arms and legs were ready to drop off when he reached home, his head ached and he had had nothing to eat all day but some dry rotis and water. That day, too, his father threw his hard-earned, precious one rupee into the well.

The third day Ashok had to go to a farm on the other side of a hill. He climbed the hill, worked and returned home late at night, too tired to even eat dinner.

He went to his father and gave the coin. When his father was about to get up and go to the courtyard to throw the coin into the well, Ashok could stay quiet no longer.

'Do you even know how hard I had to work to earn this money? I had to walk up a steep hill, sow seeds in a massive field in the hot sun, the farmer's dog hated me and barked at me the whole day, I had to milk the cows in the evening and one kicked me right here—here on my buttocks—and the hens pecked at me when I went into the coop, and while I was walking back, it was so dark I slipped and fell into a pool of mud and got bitten by at least a million mosquitoes . . . And now you are throwing the money I earned after such hardships into the well? You, who have never stepped out of his comfortable room to even see what the world is like outside? I cannot let you throw this money into the well, even if it is only a rupee.'

Ashok stopped for breath, and was surprised to see his father smiling. Then Ramnath said, 'My son, you have finally realized how hard it is to earn even the smallest sum. Now you know the effort one has to put in to bring home an honest day's wage. I think you are ready to start off on your own. I will help you in your business. Never forget the virtues of hard work and honesty.'

Ashok smiled and nodded. He had learnt a very valuable lesson from his wise father.

The Bird with Golden Wings

Varsha lived with her mother, who worked as a cook in a rich man's house. Every evening, her mother returned from work with a little rice, which she would then cook for herself and her daughter. Varsha and her mother lived happily enough, satisfied with what they had.

One evening, Varsha's mother brought home some extra rice. Before leaving the next morning, she cleaned it and spread it on a mat to dry in the terrace. Then she called Varsha and said, 'Sit here and see that no bird pecks at the rice. I will cook this for us when I return in the evening.' Varsha sat down by the rice with a little stick in her hand. After a while, a tiny sparrow came hopping by. It looked hungrily at the grains. Varsha took pity on it and gave it a few grains. The bird ate those and flew away. Then an old crow came and cawed loudly beside her. 'I'm hungry!' it seemed to say. So Varsha gave it some grains too, and it flew away after eating them. Then, the strangest thing happened.

A big bird with shining golden wings came and perched next to her. It was clearly very old. The bird looked at the rice spread out on the mat. Then it spoke in a beautiful voice, 'Will you give me some rice too?' Varsha was very surprised. 'Go ahead,' she said, 'but take only a few grains, or else my mother will scold me.'

The old bird hopped forward and, in an instant, gulped down all the rice! Varsha looked in dismay at the empty mat. What would her mother say? 'Why did you do that?' she asked the bird. It bent its head and said softly, 'I'm sorry. I was hungry and could not stop myself. But don't

worry, come with me to my house in the big banyan tree and I'll give you something which will make your mother forget her anger.'

The banyan tree was just outside the village, and it was nearly evening. Varsha was scared. But she knew she would have to go so her mother would have something to eat when she returned home after a hard day's work. She went with the bird. When they reached the tree, Varsha saw there was a little golden house on top of the tree. How strange that she hadn't noticed that before, she thought. The bird spread out its long golden wings and flew easily to the house at the top of the tree. But how would Varsha reach there?

The bird called down, 'Tell me, what kind of ladder do you want?' Varsha was puzzled. She knew of only one kind of ladder. 'A light bamboo one,' she called out. Out of nowhere, a sturdy ladder made of bamboo appeared before her and she climbed up the tree. When she walked into the bird's house, she saw everything was golden. The chairs, tables, plates and glasses were all made of gold!

Varsha sat on a golden chair and the bird said, 'You

must be hungry. I will give you something to eat. Tell me, what kind of plate would you want to eat from?' Varsha thought hard. She always ate from a banana leaf which her mother picked and cleaned for her. It made the food more tasty, she thought. 'A banana leaf, please,' she told her bird friend.

In a moment, a nice green banana leaf appeared before her full of delicious food. Varsha ate up all the food. The bird now placed three boxes in front of her. 'These boxes contain the price of the grains that I ate up,' it said. 'Choose any one to take back with you.' Varsha was embarrassed. After all, the bird had only eaten the few grains that had been left and, besides, she had a long way to walk back home. So she pointed to the smallest box. 'Can I have this one, please?'

'Of course. There you go,' said the golden bird, handing Varsha the small box.

Varsha thanked the bird many times, climbed down the ladder and went home.

There her mother was anxiously waiting for her. Varsha told her all about her adventures, and together they opened the box. It was filled with precious stones. Now her mother would no longer need to work in the rich man's house. She could open a little shop and whatever they earned would be enough for the two of them. The people of the village were surprised to find Varsha and her mother so well off all of a sudden. Nosy, quarrelsome Kapila was most curious and was bursting to know how her poor, simple neighbours had suddenly become rich. Unable to contain herself, she went and asked Varsha's mother, who told her the entire story.

Kapila realized here was a way for her to become rich too. Next day, she sat on her terrace with a basket full of grain in front of her. When the sparrow and the crow hopped up, she shooed them away loudly. Soon, the golden bird came. Kapila offered it all the rice in the basket.

'I want only a few grains,' the bird replied.

'All right, all right,' interrupted Kapila rudely. 'But remember, you will have to pay for it.' The bird agreed and invited Kapila to its house in the banyan tree.

Happily, Kapila went with the bird. When she stood below the tree, the bird asked, 'What kind of ladder do you want?' Kapila said, 'A golden one, of course!' thinking she could take it back with her too.

A golden ladder appeared before her. Kapila heaved herself up the ladder and entered the golden house.

'What plate do you want to eat in?' asked the bird. 'Obviously a golden one!' Kapila said with a happy cackle. When the food came, she gobbled it all down. The bird now set before her three boxes and asked her to choose one as the price for the grain. Greedy Kapila chose the largest one. She stuffed it into the bag she had brought with her, along with the plate, and without a word of thanks, dashed down the ladder. Then she lugged the ladder all the way back to her house.

As soon as she reached home, she pulled the plate and box out of her bag. But the plate was now an ordinary banana leaf! She looked at the ladder. It had turned into a rickety old bamboo ladder. She opened the box. A large black cobra shot out and hissed at her. Kapila dropped everything and ran and ran. When she finally gathered up her courage and returned home many hours later, the box, ladder and plate had disappeared.

The bird with golden wings never appeared in the village again.

The Smartest Cook

Shekhar was a very clever young man.

One day, he saw some people in his village excitedly discussing something. Shekhar walked up and heard them talking about Narayan, the village landlord. 'It is impossible to meet Narayan. He never agrees to meet any of us, and he is so shrewd that we cannot even go to his house and surprise him.'

Shekhar listened for a while. Then he piped up, 'What is so difficult about this? You watch! Not only will I go and meet him, he will even invite me to have breakfast with him.'

Everyone burst out laughing at this bold announcement. 'Go on then, Shekhar, let us see you do this. We bet a thousand rupees you will not be able to keep your word.'

Next morning, Shekhar landed up at the landlord's house. The hefty guards at the gate refused to let him enter. But Shekhar was calm. He said to them, 'Go

and tell your master I have come to talk about gold bricks.'

When Narayan heard this from one of his guards, he was curious. He was having breakfast and invited Shekhar to join him. After all, he had to be nice to someone offering him gold bricks!

While having breakfast Narayan asked, 'What is the weight of the gold brick?'

'It depends on the size.'

'What is the price?'

'It depends on the weight.'

'How many gold bricks can you bring?'

'As many as you want.'

'When can you bring them?'

'Whenever you want them.'

Narayan was impressed. 'How many gold bricks do you have?'

By now Shekhar had eaten his fill of the soft, white idlis and steaming sambar. 'I don't have any,' he replied, burping and washing his hands.

Narayan was furious. 'Then why did you say you wanted to talk to me about gold bricks?'

'That's what I did, didn't I? I talked to you about gold bricks. Did I ever say I had the bricks?'

'Throw this man out,' Narayan shouted. 'He is a cheat!'

'Sir, please don't worry. I will go my own.'

Shekhar walked away. The other villagers had to give him the thousand rupees they had promised.

A few days later, Shekhar was travelling to another village. He came across a group of villagers standing in the middle of the road, murmuring, 'We need a strong man to move this huge rock from the road.'

Shekhar stood there for a minute, and then he said, 'I will do it for you. But give me a thousand rupees first.'

Looking at Shekhar, who was as thin as a stick, the villagers were doubtful. But the headman was ready to take the risk. He said, 'We will pay you half the amount now and the other half after the work is done.'

Shekhar agreed. He put five hundred rupees in his pocket. Then he bent and stood with his back to the huge rock. Everyone stared at him in astonishment. The headman asked, 'Why are you not moving the rock?'

'I am waiting for someone to place this rock on my back so I can run and keep it wherever you want me to.'

The villagers realized they had been tricked.

Shekhar left them, smiling, with five hundred rupees in his pocket.

The next day he went to another village. The annual village sports day was being held. A hefty man with bulging muscles was taking up challenges thrown by the crowd. One person came with a towel in his hand. 'Throw the towel in such a way that it falls on or behind that wall. I will give a thousand rupees as prize if you can do it.'

The wall was at a great distance. The muscleman took the towel and threw it hard, but the towel just flapped gently in the breeze and settled down on the grass in front of the wall.

Now Shekhar came forward. Seeing this skinny boy take up the challenge which had defeated the strongest person in the village, everyone burst out laughing. Quietly, Shekhar picked up the towel and tied a stone to one end. Then he

threw it and, weighted with the stone, the towel went sailing beyond the wall.

Shekhar collected his prize.

The king of that kingdom was very fond of good food. One day he announced, 'I want to find the best cook in this kingdom. Whoever brings me the tastiest food will get a reward.'

The best cooks in the kingdom whipped up mouth-watering dishes for the king. Plates piled high with aromatic biryani, fat slices of sweet fish and tender vegetables floating in delicate gravies were presented before the king. But the king would put only a few morsels in his mouth and say, 'Hmmm.' He was yet to find the best cook in his kingdom.

Shekhar walked into the palace and said, 'Your Majesty, I can bring you the best dish in the world. But to eat that your tongue must be clean.'

'What do you mean by that?' the king demanded.

'You must not use your tongue to taste anything before you eat the meal that I serve you.'

The king agreed, eager to taste the best food in his kingdom.

The next day he refused to eat anything, for fear of making his tongue unclean. As a result, he had to skip his breakfast, lunch and tea-time snack. By dinner time, the king was tired and very, very hungry. He was waiting for Shekhar to appear with his wonderful meal, counting the minutes till his dinner was served.

Soon, Shekhar respectfully placed before the king a bowlful of plain boiled white rice with some salt on the side. The courtiers were all shocked. But the king was ready to eat anything that was placed before him.

'I can't wait any longer. Give that to me!'

He snatched the bowl from Shekhar's hand and finished off every grain of rice in a hurry. Then he sat back and wiped his mouth in satisfaction.

Shekhar asked, 'How was the food, Your Majesty?'

'I have never tasted anything better, but . . .'

'Then give me my reward.'

'You only gave me rice and salt! That is not what the best cook in the kingdom can serve.'

'It is not important what I served, Your Majesty. What matters is how much you enjoyed the meal.'

'You told me not to taste anything before the meal, so I was hungry. And that is why the rice tasted so good,' protested the king.

'I'm sorry, Your Majesty. You said yourself that you have never tasted anything better. So I should get that prize.'

The king realized he had been outsmarted by Shekhar. He liked this young man's sense of humour and his ready wit. He advised him: 'Shekhar, you are a very intelligent person. Use your brains for better things, and one day you will become very famous.'

Shekhar listened to the king and decided to use his unusual intelligence to study hard. And one day, he became the king's favourite minister and helped him do a lot of good work for the kingdom.

Sukeshini and the Lake Demon

Sukeshini lived in a small village near a mountain. For many years her village had been facing a drought. All the streams and ponds had dried up. The villagers had to walk long distances to fetch a bucket of water. Their crops suffered as there was no rain to irrigate them. The villagers lived in great hardship.

Sukeshini was very beautiful, with unusually long hair that swept the ground when she left it open. She stayed in a little mud hut with her mother. They had some sheep.

It was Sukeshini's responsibility to graze the sheep. Every day she had to climb higher and higher up the mountainside as it was all parched and dusty. One day, nearly halfway up the mountain, she found a lone tree growing. Exhausted, she sat down to rest under its shade. As she sat there, looking around her, she noticed a creeper with fresh, new leaves climbing up the side of the tree. Thinking she could pluck some leaves and

give them to her sheep, she pulled at the leaves. But they would not come off, so she tugged harder and harder, till, to her surprise, a huge pumpkin came out from under the ground! And along with the pumpkin gushed out sweet, cool water. She had discovered a hidden stream! Joyfully, Sukeshini drank the water and bathed in it. Her village's water problem would finally be solved.

Just as she was about to make her way back to her

village, there was a whirlwind. It picked her up and carried her all the way to the top of the mountain. She also realized that the pumpkin had rolled and stopped at the mouth of the fountain, from where the water was gushing forth.

The whirlwind threw her down on the mountaintop. As Sukeshini recovered her breath, she found herself beside a beautiful blue lake. And in the clear water of the lake, she saw the reflection of a huge, angry demon, who was staring at her. She looked up in terror. The demon was covered all over with black hair, his nails were as long as her arms and his head towered into the clouds. He was terribly angry.

'How dare a little chit of a girl like you drink from my hidden stream?' he screamed. 'I am the master of this mountain, and this lake and the stream belong to me. I share this water with no one. If you are thinking of going back to your village and telling everyone there about these two sources of water, forget it. If anyone comes looking for the lake and the stream, I will find you and drown you in this lake. That long, black hair will be forever underwater. Remember that!'

Then the whirlwind came rushing up again, picked up Sukeshini and flung her back to her village. Everything had happened so quickly that Sukeshini wondered if it was all a dream. But then she found a little leaf from the creeper stuck in her hair and knew that it had all really happened: she had found water, and then a demon had found her!

For many days after this she remained deep in thought. She saw all around her the hardship the people of her village were facing. Women walked miles every day looking for water, leaving their hungry children at home. The men could not work in their fields. Everyone was getting poorer and poorer. As the days passed, Sukeshini remained silent. Her beautiful black hair turned grey with worry.

One night, her mother had a fever. As Sukeshini wiped her hot brow, she wished she had a little water to wash her mother's hot forehead with and that she could give her a drink of the sweet water she had tasted in the mountain. Suddenly she realized she could stay silent no longer. She could not watch everyone suffer, knowing there was a source of water so close by.

The next morning she called a group of young men and women together. She told them the entire story—of how she had found water, the terrifying whirlwind and, finally, the hideous demon that lived on top of the mountain. Then she said, 'I want some of you to come with me. I will show you how to get to the stream. When it gushes out, you must direct it to the village. Don't worry about me. I will happily meet my fate at the hands of the demon.'

A young man in the crowd stood up and said, 'Sukeshini, do not give up your life for us. If we put our heads together, we can find a way to trick the demon. Creatures so large are often not the smartest. I have an idea. We will make a wooden doll which looks just like you. You shave off all your hair and give it to me. I will attach it to the doll. Without your hair, you will be unrecognizable to the demon. He will pick up the doll and drown it instead of you.'

Everyone agreed this was a clever plan. The carpenter made a doll that looked just like Sukeshini. The barber shaved her hair. And the young man expertly fixed it on

the doll's
head. Then
it was dressed
in Sukeshini's
clothes, and from
a distance no one
could make out that it
was not a live girl.

Carrying it between
them, a large group of
villagers followed Sukeshini up
the mountain. She soon found the lone
tree with the creeper growing around it. She
told them where to
pull, and how

hard. But before they started tugging at the creeper, she made them dig a canal that would channel the water from the stream straight into their village.

The villagers dug happily, then they pulled the creeper just as Sukeshini had told them to. And sure enough, up popped the enormous pumpkin, followed by a gush of the sweetest, coolest water they had ever tasted. It rushed down the canal they had dug, and reached their parched village. And in the same instant, the demon unleashed his terrible whirlwind to pick up Sukeshini and punish her.

The whirlwind came howling down at the group of villagers. It swept up the doll and flung it into the lake, where it sank to the bottom. But Sukeshini's long hair floated up. It carried the water from the lake down in a waterfall to the village. The village was now blessed with two new sources of water.

When the demon realized that the villagers had played a trick on him, he was very angry. He stamped up and down the mountaintop for many days. Finally, he decided to leave so no one would come to know how he had been tricked.

Sukeshini's village prospered with the water gushing back to their fields and tanks. And in the course of time, her hair grew back—as black and beautiful as ever.

The Silly Rich Boy

Manjunath was a rich landlord and Anil was his only son. Anil grew up not having to do a spot of work, surrounded by all kinds of comforts. He was selfish and headstrong.

One day, Manjunath decided to sell one of his cows. He prepared to leave for the market. Anil watched him get ready and said, 'Let me take the cow and sell it.'

Manjunath looked at his son and said, 'You have never done business before. Why don't you accompany me this time and watch how I go about it, and then you can start doing it on your own?'

But Anil was adamant. 'I don't need to watch you, Father!' he grumbled. 'It's just a matter of selling a cow, not something that requires me to be a pundit or spend years studying!'

Manjunath saw his son's lips were pursed and his shoulders set in a way that usually meant he would not listen to reason. He sighed. Perhaps if he allowed Anil to go alone and get cheated, his stubborn son would learn a lesson. So he said aloud, 'All right, then. Go.'

Anil rushed out and brought the most splendid horse from the stables. He dressed in his best clothes, with a gold chain around his neck and rings on his fingers, and jumped up to sit on the horse. Manjunath intervened mildly, 'When you go to do business, it's best not to show how rich you already are . . .'

But Anil gave no heed to his father's words. With an arrogant toss of his head he took one end of the cow's rope and trotted off on his grand horse.

As he rode by, his clothes and jewellery shining in the sun, his beautiful horse tossing its mane and the plump cow following behind, he passed three men. These three men understood that this silly rich boy was going to the market to sell the cow, and they decided to cheat him.

The first said, 'I will take his cow.'

Another said, 'I'll take his horse.'

The third man said, 'And I'll take his clothes and jewels.'

They followed Anil for some time. Then they quietly slipped the rope from around the cow's head and tied only a bell to it. Foolish Anil did not realize that the cow was gone and he was leading only a bell by the rope. After some time, when he finally got down to rest, he noticed that the cow was gone. He was very worried, and started looking around. The second cheater now came up to him.

'What is it, brother?' he asked in his friendliest voice. 'Have you lost something?'

'I'm looking for my cow.'

'Was it a white cow with a black tail?'

'Yes! That's the one! Where did you see it?'

The man pointed in the opposite direction and said, 'I saw a man going that way with it. If you give me your horse, I'll catch up with him in no time and bring him back to you.'

This seemed like a good idea to Anil and he quickly agreed. The second cheater rode away on the horse, never to show his face again. Anil sat by the road waiting for him to return. The hours passed by but there was no sign of the man, horse or cow.

When it was evening, Anil started to walk back home. He passed by a well. The third cheater was sitting by the well pretending to be very worried. He jumped up and came to Anil. 'Help me, sir! I am a diamond merchant. I was drawing some water from the well when my box of diamonds slipped and fell into the water. I cannot swim, and if I don't get the box, I will lose all my life's savings.'

Anil thought quickly, 'I have already lost my horse and cow. If I help this man in return for some money, Father will see I have earned more money than I would have by selling a stupid cow and will forgive me.' So he said aloud, 'I will help you. But you must pay me twenty gold coins.'

The cheater nodded quickly. 'Here are ten coins. When you get back my diamonds, I'll give you ten more. Now hurry! Jump into the well and find the box!' Anil quickly took off his grand clothes and jewels and placed them in a pile by the well. He placed the ten gold coins on top. Then he took a deep breath and dived into the water. He searched and searched for the box but, of course, found nothing except some copper coins and other rubbish passersby had tossed into the well. When he finally came out, there was no sign of the man, neither was there any sign of his belongings. Poor Anil had to walk home in his underwear, and the entire village laughed at his stupidity.

The Clever Thieves

Kampali was a prosperous city. The only problem the city faced was occasional thefts.

The city was home to some really clever thieves who made merry even when the king placed many guards all over town. One of the cleverest thieves was Ramu.

One night, when Ramu was out on the streets looking for a good place to burgle, he noticed another man walking down the street. There's a saying that it takes one thief to recognize another, and Ramu immediately guessed that they were of the same profession. The other man's name was Bheemu. The two got talking, and soon they were recounting to each other their most daring exploits. Finally Ramu said, 'If you can prove yourself as clever as me, we can become partners and carry out bigger thefts. We will earn more and divide the money.'

Bheemu smiled. 'But how will we know who is cleverer?' he asked. They decided to spend the night thinking about this. The next morning, they went to the jewellers' street in the bazaar. This street was lined with jewellery shops. The two thieves spotted a wealthy-looking man, wearing a fancy red turban, examining the ornaments displayed in a shop window. 'Watch me,' Ramu whispered. 'I'll steal his purse and he will be none the wiser.'

He casually walked up to the man and, while pretending to admire the ornaments, picked the man's pocket as silently as a shadow, returning with a fat purse jingling with coins. When they opened it, the two thieves counted ten gold coins. 'Now it's your turn,' challenged Ramu. 'Show me you can do something cleverer than this.'

'Easy!' shrugged Bheemu. 'Watch how I prove the owner of this purse is a thief.' He removed two gold coins from the pouch and replaced them with copper coins. Then he quietly glided up to the man, dropped the purse back in his pocket and clutching his arm, started shouting, 'Thief! Thief! This man has stolen my purse!'

The innocent man was alarmed. 'Of course I'm not a thief,' he shouted.

'You are, you are!' Bheemu yelled. 'I can prove that my purse is in your pocket. It is brown in colour and there are eight gold coins and two copper coins in it.'

'Then it's easy to prove myself,' the man answered. 'My purse is also brown, but I have ten gold coins in it . . . See, here it is!' And he pulled out the purse to show everyone. But to his horror, when they counted the coins, there were eight gold and two copper coins! The crowd started raining blows on the innocent man for stealing, and Bheemu walked away victoriously with the purse and all the coins in full view of the entire market.

Ramu and Bheemu became fast friends and partners in crime so that they could pool their cunning and pull off even more daring thefts. They decided to burgle nothing less than the royal treasury. There were many guards in front of the treasury door, so Ramu made a hole in the roof. The two slid down from there, helped themselves to all kinds of treasures and slipped out the same way. They closed the hole carefully behind them.

The next morning the entire court was in uproar! The city's thieves had become too daring! They had stolen from the treasury! While everyone was scratching their heads trying to understand how the thieves had done it, the king's wise old minister suggested, 'They must have surely dug a hole somewhere to come in and covered it up on their way out. The best way to find the location of the hole is to close the room and fill it with smoke. If we see the smoke escaping, it will show us where the hole was made.'

Sure enough, when they did this, they found that a hole had been made in the roof. The minister had a plan to catch the thieves. 'I am sure there were two of them,' he said. 'Let's not tell anyone about this. Now that they have discovered a way to get into the treasury, they will try again. I have an idea. Keep a drum of glue right under the hole, where the first thief will fall in. He will get stuck. The other one will escape, but we will catch him after questioning the one we catch.'

The king ordered that this plan be carried out. When Ramu and Bheemu came to steal again, Ramu got stuck in the barrel of glue. He told his friend, 'You run. I will not tell them anything about you.'

Bheemu was as cool as a cucumber. 'Don't worry, Ramu. Here, have this medicine. It will make you sleep and slow your heartbeat so much that people will think you are dead. After that, leave it to me to rescue you.'

Bheemu escaped after giving the medicine to Ramu. By the time the king's guards stormed into the treasury, they found only Ramu, lying in the drum, looking quite dead.

The minister suggested, 'We'll keep the dead body outside the doors of the fort. We'll place many guards around it, and as soon as someone comes to claim the body, we'll know he was this thief's friend.' So they placed Ramu outside the fort, and the soldiers waited for someone to come. But no one did.

When it was getting dark, an old man walked up, pushing a creaking cart filled with jugs of wine. He hobbled up to the bored soldiers and said, 'Will you please help me push this cart? I am old, and these jugs of wine are heavy. I'll give you one jug as payment.'

The soldiers refused. 'Can't you see this body lying here? It is a very important body. He is a dangerous criminal. We cannot leave the body for even a minute. Go on now, old man.'

The man, who was really Bheemu in disguise, said in a sad, feeble voice, 'All right then. If you would rather guard a corpse than help a weak, elderly man . . .' And he started pushing his cart up the road. The soldiers now felt bad. They also wanted the wine that they could hear sloshing around in the jugs. 'No one has come to claim this corpse today. How does it matter if we leave it for a few minutes and help an old man?' they told each other.

They went up to the cart and started pushing it. Bheemu gave them one jug of wine, in which he had mixed a sleeping medicine. The soldiers drank it and fell down in a heap, snoring loudly. Bheemu hurried up to where Ramu was lying and gave him a dose of another medicine to wake him up from his death-like sleep. No sooner was the medicine poured into his mouth than Ramu awoke as good as new. He dashed off, taking the cart with him, and Bheemu, still dressed as an old man, lay down among the soldiers, pretending to be fast asleep.

The next day the king found all the soldiers snoring and the dead body gone. Bheemu, too, woke up when the others were shaken awake, and pretended to lament the loss of his cart of wine. 'Your magic dead body cast a spell on all of us and stole my cart. It was my one and only possession. Oh, how will I make a living without it!' he wailed loud and long.

The king's men shooed him away. 'Off with you! All this is your fault. Go, before we lock you in jail.'

Bheemu walked away from there, sniffing about his lost cart.

This time the wise minister could think of no other clever plan to catch the thieves. 'They seem to have studied the craft of thieving very closely!' he remarked. 'My suggestion is, Your Majesty, to make an announcement saying they are pardoned, and they can work for you, helping you solve cases of burglary and other crimes.'

The king did just that. Ramu and Bheemu, who were by now bored of being thieves, joined the king's service. This is how the king caught the cleverest thieves in his kingdom: by turning them into policemen, who served him honestly for many, many years. It was that easy!

The King with Donkey's Ears

King Parikshit had a large kingdom where everything was available in plenty. His enemies were too afraid to attack because of his huge army. His people were happy as he was just and noble. All his subjects sang his praises and loved him dearly.

But the king was not happy. He had a dark secret, and he always feared that the secret would be revealed. The secret was that the king's ears were shaped just like a donkey's! Large and hairy, they stuck straight up over his head. Anyone looking at him would be charmed by his looks—his handsome nose and honey-brown eyes—not knowing about his donkey ears!

Parikshit's donkey ears were a top secret. From the time he was a small boy, his mother had covered his ears with a turban, and he continued to wear one even after he became king. As a result, the only people who knew about them were his parents, who were now dead, and his barber, Somu. After all, it is rather difficult to get a haircut with a turban on your head.

Somu had been sworn to secrecy by the Queen Mother herself, and he never dreamt of betraying that trust. But when he became old and frail, and was no longer able to walk to the palace and give the king his haircut, he decided to send his son, Dinesh, as the king's new barber. And so he had to tell him about the secret.

Dinesh was a good boy, very obedient, and listened to his father's words carefully. 'Dinesh, be careful,' said Somu. 'A great secret will be revealed to you today when you start cutting the king's hair. But it is a secret our family has vowed never to tell anyone. You must never ever talk about it to another human being, else a horrible punishment will be handed down to you and me.' Dinesh promised never to tell anyone what he learnt at the palace that day.

Soon he was in the king's presence. The king sat on the royal haircutting chair. The guards closed and barred the doors and windows of the room and stayed outside. The king looked around carefully, then slowly took off his turban. And there, revealed in all their glory, were those horrible donkey ears.

Dinesh could not believe his eyes. How could these terrible ears belong to their beloved, handsome king?

Why, just yesterday he had heard a new song composed by the royal bard extolling the king's divine good looks! Then he understood—this must be the secret his father had been going on about. This is what he could never talk about to another soul.

Poor Dinesh. He went home that day, ate his dinner and lay down in bed. But he could not sleep. All he could see whenever he closed his eyes were those large donkey ears. He tossed and turned all night. He felt his stomach beginning to bloat; he just had to spill this secret. 'If I don't tell someone, I am going to burst!' he thought desperately. Finally, when it was nearly time for the sun to rise, he could no longer control himself.

While the whole world slept, Dinesh sneaked out of his house. Carefully, he looked around to see if anyone was about. No, the whole town was sleeping deeply. He walked quietly to a field by the side of the road. Some pits had been dug there to plant saplings. He tiptoed to one pit, shoved his face into the mud and shouted, 'The king's ears are like donkeys' ears, that is why he always wears a turban . . . the king's ears are like donkeys' ears . . . the king's ears are like donkeys' ears . . .'

As soon as he had shouted this out, he felt his stomach become normal again. Relieved, he covered up the pit with mud, planted a sapling in it and went home and lay down on his bed. Soon, he was fast asleep.

Some years went by. The little sapling planted in the pit where Dinesh had shouted grew into a sturdy tree. Meanwhile, the king decided to marry. He wanted to find the most beautiful, most sensible bride. So he decided to send the royal messenger around the kingdom to announce the king's search for a bride.

The town crier went to the royal carpenter and asked him to make some new drums. He wanted strong drums which would make a loud sound as he made this most important announcement. The royal carpenter said that he would find the best wood available in the kingdom to fashion these drums, and set off to find a suitable tree. As he walked down the road, he looked at the trees planted by the roadside. One tree looked particularly strong and sturdy. He decided to use the wood from that tree for the new drums.

He cut the wood and made the drum. The leaves of the tree lay scattered on the road. A passing shepherd saw them and thought, 'Why are these fresh, green leaves lying on the road? Let me take them home for my sheep.' He gathered the leaves into three large bundles and set off for home. On the way he met a cowherd.

'Brother, you have three large bundles of green leaves, can you spare one for my cow here?' the cowherd asked the shepherd.

Generously, the shepherd gave him one bag. As he walked on, he met a mahout on an elephant. 'Brother, you have two large bundles of green leaves, can you spare one for my elephant here?' asked the mahout. The shepherd gave him a bundle of leaves too.

By now, the royal carpenter had made the new drum. The town crier set off happily with it. He reached the middle of the town and in the busy marketplace started beating his new drum. But what was this! Instead of the usual 'dum dum' noise, words were coming from the drum! When the people listened carefully, they heard the words clearly: 'The king's ears are like donkeys' ears, that is why he always wears a turban . . . the king's ears are like donkeys' ears . . . the king's ears are like donkeys' ears . . .'

Before these words wafted into the air and could float away, the sheep, cow and elephant which had eaten the leaves of the tree opened their mouths, and instead of a baa, moo and trumpet, these words were heard: 'The king's ears are like donkeys' ears, that is why he always wears a turban . . . the king's ears are like donkeys' ears . . . the king's ears are like donkeys' ears . . .'

Thus, the entire city came to know the king's secret without Dinesh telling anybody.

Books for the Cook

Aditya was a scholarly king. He was well versed in all forms of learning and held scholars in the highest regard. He believed scholars should be provided with all the help they may need so that they could pursue their studies without worrying about money. He identified some learned people in his kingdom and gave them quite a lot of money, and they spent all their time reading and learning.

Charvaka was one such person. He lived in a remote corner of the kingdom, yet was famous for his knowledge and wisdom. With the money he got from the king, he built a large school where he trained many gifted students. The school was comfortable, with all kinds of luxuries and many servants to look after the students' every need.

Some years after starting this school, Charvaka died and his disciple, Shantanu, looked after the school now. He was a bright student once, but living in luxury had made him lazy. He now only thought of leisure and comfort and had not opened a book for many months. After all, the king's money was always there if they needed anything.

Meanwhile, King Aditya decided to test the scholars to whom he was providing his patronage. He sent out a letter to them with a list of questions, inviting them to come to the court to provide the answers. The questions were:

What is the depth of the sea?

How many stars are there in the sky?

What is permanent?

When Shantanu received the letter he was at his wits' end. He had no idea what the answers were! He had certainly not learnt any of this in the few books he had read recently. He sat sadly, thinking he would no longer be able to stay as the head of the school and, more importantly, would have to give up the comfortable life he was leading. He was so worried, he stopped eating.

In the school's kitchen, there worked a clever cook. His name was Dhirendra. Whenever he got some free time he would sit in the library and read as many books as he could. Seeing the dishes he prepared for Shantanu coming back uneaten, he decided to find out what the matter was. The master had not touched even his favourite laddoos in the last few days!

Shantanu showed him the letter and told him his worries. Dhirendra read the questions and said, 'Don't worry, guruji. I'll go to the king dressed like you and answer these questions. Nothing will happen to you or the school.'

Shantanu did not know whether he should trust a simple cook to answer such deep philosophical questions, but he had little choice. So he agreed. He gave Dhirendra his scholar's robe to wear when he appeared before the king. Dhirendra reached the court on the appointed day and introduced himself as Shantanu. The king and the courtiers looked at his sober scholar's gown and believed he was indeed the scholar. 'So, tell me,' questioned the king in his deepest voice, 'have you got the answers to my three questions?'

'Yes indeed, Your Majesty,' Dhirendra bowed and replied. 'The sea is as deep as the depth to which a stone can sink. There are 1,11,12,222 stars in the sky. If you don't believe me, count them for yourself and check. And the only thing in life that does not change is Truth. It does not change with time. It is not always easy to tell the truth, and the person telling it and the person hearing it should be courageous.'

The king was very pleased with these answers. 'A thousand gold coins to this school!' he announced.

Now Dhirendra removed his robe—underneath he was dressed in the simple garb of a cook. 'Your Majesty, I spoke about the importance of Truth, so I have to make a confession. I am not a scholar or a teacher. I am a humble cook working in the kitchens of this school. Our head scholar did not know the answers to the questions and was afraid to appear before you. So, I offered to come in his place and give you the answers, to save the school. I tried to dupe you. I am ready to face any punishment that you may decide to give me.'

The king was furious. So this was how the learned people of his kingdom behaved! A cook was better than all the scholars put together. 'Off with Shantanu!' he shouted. 'He is removed from the position of head scholar and in his place I appoint Dhirendra. And no more money for these schools either!'

Dhirendra folded his hands and said, 'Your Majesty, if I may make a suggestion. When men receive money without working for it they don't appreciate it. They become lazy and arrogant. I am not learned enough to be a teacher. I will work hard and become a teacher one day. But till then I will remain a cook, reading books in my spare time. You could support the schools as you did earlier, but with less money, so they understand its value.'

The king was pleased with this suggestion. He let Shantanu continue as the head of the school but kept a strict watch over how the money was spent and often visited the school to check on the progress of the students. Shantanu, too, did not shirk his duties any more. And Dhirendra continued reading the best books in the land till he became a teacher one day.

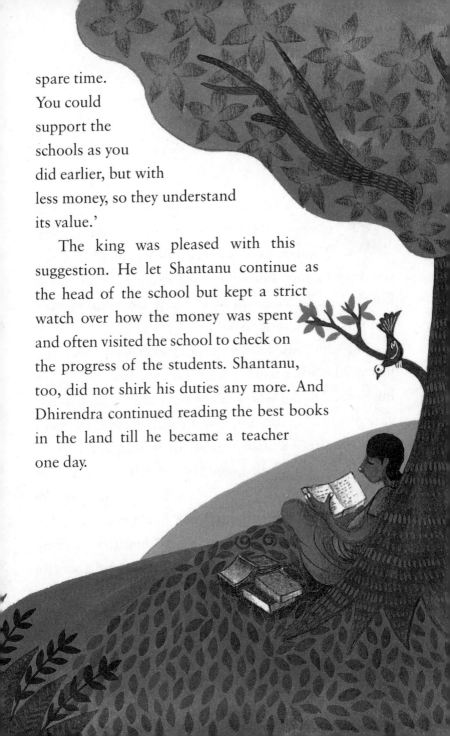

The Kind Stepmother

Jaya was a young woman, married to a widower. Her husband already had a son. Though Jaya was the boy's stepmother, she was very fond of him and looked after him very well. But the boy, Badri, could never accept her as his mother and was always rude to her.

Jaya's husband fell very ill, and soon it was clear that he would not live much longer. Jaya promised her dying husband, 'Do not worry about Badri. I will always take care of him. We did not have a child of our own, but I will look after him like he is my own son.'

Jaya's husband died, and she was left all alone with the boy. They were poor and had to somehow make ends meet. To add to her misery, Badri became ruder. Where earlier his father would stop him from talking back to Jaya, he now did whatever he wanted and said anything that came to his mind. He would not help Jaya with the chores and instead spent whatever little

money she managed to earn in buying useless things. His stepmother did not know what to do with him.

In Jaya's garden, there lived a snake, which she treated like her own child. The snake came to visit her in the kitchen every night and she would feed it a bowl of milk. The snake would drink the milk and go away quietly.

One day, she did not have the money to buy milk. She waited sadly for the snake to come that night, and as soon as it slithered in, she cried out, 'Oh my child, I can't feed you tonight. I had no money to buy milk.'

To her surprise, the snake spoke to her in a human voice. 'Don't worry. You can cut an inch off my tail. By tomorrow morning it will turn into gold. You can use it to buy anything you wish.'

Jaya was amazed to hear the snake speak. She was even more shocked by what it said. 'No, no,' she said. 'You are like a child to me. How can I cut your body? I don't want gold that comes from hurting you.'

The snake swayed a bit and then replied, 'You have looked after me for so long. No one bothers to feed us, they only look at us with fear. You have given me love.

Don't worry about cutting my tail. I will not be hurt, and my tail will grow back in no time.'

Hearing these words, Jaya reluctantly agreed and cut off a little bit of the snake's tail. The next morning, when she woke up, to her amazement she found that it had indeed turned to gold! She sold the gold, and after a long time there was plenty of food in the house. She even had some money left over after buying all that she'd needed.

As Jaya's household prospered, so did Badri's extravagance. He used up all the extra money in the house. When the money finished, the snake saw Jaya's sad face and told her to cut off some more of its tail.

The days passed in this way. Badri tried hard to find out where his stepmother got the money from, but he could never guess. One day, he decided to keep a close watch on her through the entire day. They had no money again, and Jaya had not been able to buy anything. As night fell, she went to her kitchen and sat there, silent tears rolling down her cheeks. Badri peeked from a little hole in the door.

After some time a large snake slithered into the kitchen. As Badri watched in surprise, the snake said something to his stepmother. Then she picked up a knife and cut off a little bit of its tail! She hid it in a purse where he knew she kept all the money. Now he understood where the money was coming from. An evil idea crept into Badri's head.

The next night, he took one of Jaya's saris when she was out of the house. As night fell, he locked her in another room, draped the sari around himself and sat in the kitchen with the sari pulled low over his face. He placed a bowl of milk in front of him and waited for the snake to appear. Sure enough, after a while, the snake came in, and headed straight for the bowl. As it lapped up the milk, Badri quickly stole around it, whipped out a knife and cut off a large portion of the snake's tail. Blood spurted out of the wound, and the hurt snake now understood that the person in the sari was someone else. It lashed out at Badri and said, 'You are a greedy man. You never learnt how to be a good person like your stepmother. With a little bit of my tail she got some gold, which would have been enough for the two of you. But you were not satisfied and cut off such a large portion of my tail. Now, to teach you a lesson, I will never come back here again. You will have to work hard and earn money for yourself and your mother.'

Saying these words, the angry and hurt snake slipped away. It was never seen again. And Badri learnt that life is nothing without a little bit of kindness. He changed for the better and took up a job, looking after his stepmother to the end of her days.

Jaya never forgot the snake and every day thanked it in her prayers for changing their lives.

A Father's Wisdom

A rich and wise father had two sons, Puru and Puneet. One day, he fell seriously ill. The doctors told him he had very little time to live. So the father started putting his affairs in order. He divided his property between his two sons. Then he called them, for some last words of advice. 'Listen to me carefully, children,' he told them. 'Live by these words of mine throughout your life and you will be happy.

'Build a house in every city. Sleep comfortably. Enjoy your food. When you lend someone money, don't ask him to return it . . .'

Before he could explain his words, he died.

After his death, the two sons took their share each and settled down in different cities. Five years passed. Puru, who had been following his father's words carefully, became penniless. But his brother was richer than ever. Puru was puzzled. Both had started off with the same amount of money and had followed their father's words of advice. Yet why was he poor and his brother so rich? He decided to visit Puneet to find out.

Puneet was very pleased when Puru came to visit. He looked after him affectionately. That night, when the brothers sat down to chat after dinner, Puru asked the questions that had been playing on his mind for so many days.

'I followed Father's words exactly,' Puru said. 'I built a house in every city. But because I could not always stay there, I had to hire people to look after the houses. I lent money to people and never asked them to return it, so more and more people borrowed money from me and now I have nothing. Father said we should sleep comfortably and eat well, so I got expensive beds made and employed expert cooks to prepare my meals. All this has left me without a paisa to call my own. Yet you say you, too, have done what Father told us to do, so how are you so rich?'

Puneet smiled and said, 'Puru, you did not understand the real meaning that lay behind our father's words. When he said "build a house in every city", he meant we should make many friends living in different places, so that when we travelled to those places, these friends would offer us a place to stay and keep us comfortable.

'I, too, lent money to people and never asked them to return it. Instead, I kept a mortgage. My creditors wanted to get out of the mortgage quickly, so they would return the money as soon as they could.

'I slept comfortably each night because I would be tired after a hard day's work, and it did not matter if I were sleeping on a bed or on the hard floor.

'I ate only when hungry, and at that time the simplest meal tastes like nectar.

'Puru, you should have searched for the true meaning behind Father's words. When you say of a good-natured person, "he is like a child", you don't really mean that the person is a child, do you?'

Now Puru realized how foolish he had been. His brother gladly lent him some money to start off in life again. Having understood the true meaning of his father's advice, Puru used the money wisely and he, too, became rich and successful one day.

The Cunning Lion

 Living near a forest can lead to many adventures.

Bela lived in a tiny village which was surrounded by a thick forest. One day, a handsome young stranger arrived in her village. He said his name was Abhishek. He brought with him a basket of rare, delicious fruits. He distributed these fruits to everyone in the village, saying he had picked them while walking in the forest. The simple villagers took the fruits. Everyone liked this good-looking, generous man, especially Bela. Many young men had already asked for her hand in marriage, but Bela had rejected all the suitors. But this man was different. He walked and talked differently, almost like a king. Abhishek, too, noticed the pretty village girl and asked if she would marry him. Everyone thought it was a wonderful idea, and the wedding was fixed for a few days later. In the meanwhile, Abhishek would often disappear into the forest and return with more fruits and flowers.

The villagers sat and discussed this one day. 'These fruits are not to be found easily,' an old man told the youngsters gathered around him. 'They grow only in the remotest corners of the forest, which even people like us, who have lived here all our lives, have not been able to bring back. Abhishek is an extraordinary person, and Bela is lucky to be marrying him.'

Bela was among the young people gathered around, and heard these words. It set her thinking. How did Abhishek come and go from the farthest corners of the forest so easily? She decided to follow him and find out for herself.

That night, when the entire village was lying under its quilts and gently snoring, Bela stayed awake. Close to midnight, she spotted Abhishek making his way stealthily into the forest. She wrapped a dark shawl around her shoulders and head and followed him at a safe distance. On and on Abhishek walked, padding between the trees and bushes, as if he could see clearly in the dark. Bela stumbled a bit behind him but kept up. After all, she had grown up among these trees. Finally, Abhishek stopped in a little clearing. Then, to Bela's horror, he took a quick look around, muttered something under his breath and, in an instant, turned into a snarling, majestic lion!

He gave a mighty roar. That brought all the other animals of the forest scurrying into the clearing. Abhishek the lion then spoke in a human voice, 'Gather now, my animals. Bring to me the best and most delicious fruits from all parts of the forest. Bring me the sweetest mangoes, the tartest gooseberries, the plumpest wood apples. Bring me beautiful flowers and honey that is like nectar. Now go! Hurry!'

The tigers, bears, monkeys, squirrels and all the other animals scampered off to do as they were told. Only a huge grey elephant stood, quietly waving his trunk. He trumpeted something to the lion which Bela could not understand. But then the lion replied, in his human voice, and what he said made Bela's hair stand on end.

'You ask why I am doing this, my elephant minister? So that the people of this village, too, become my slaves, like the animals of this forest. Once I marry that foolish, proud girl, I will show them my true colours. They will provide me the best meat, do whatever I say. We will be able to eat humans whenever we want!'

Bela did not stop to hear or see any more. She turned and ran back, as fast as she could. The next morning she found Abhishek sitting in the middle of the village surrounded by the old and young alike, distributing his gifts. Where earlier she would have admired his golden brown complexion, his strong arms and royal bearing, now she could only see signs of his animal nature. Shivering, she went and told her father everything. At first he did not believe her. 'It was just a bad dream, my child,' he said, trying to calm her down. But when she insisted she had seen everything with her own eyes, he started to believe her. His daughter was brave and sensible and would never try to make him believe such a strange story for no reason.

They went to Bela's uncle and told him
the story. Together, they came up with a plan
to get rid of the impostor lion forever.
Bela's uncle used to be a wrestler and
was large and hefty, with a deep,
gruff voice. That night, Bela got
four big black blankets and two
long sticks. Then she made her
father sit on her uncle's shoulders, and she
climbed up on her father's shoulders. She
wrapped the blankets tightly around them
all. She took the two sticks and placed them
on two sides of her head. Now they looked like
a large black monster with two huge horns sticking
out of its head. They made their way to Abhishek's
hut. They stood outside and shouted out in three
different voices, 'You, lion, come out!'

Abhishek was preparing to go into the forest
and was shocked to hear a terrifying voice
address him as 'lion'. He peeped out. In the
light of the half-moon he saw a big black
creature with two horns standing at his door. He was
scared. 'W-who are you?' he asked in a shaky voice.

'I am the guardian monster of this village. Many
years ago the villagers had helped me, and I had

promised I would come to their rescue if ever they needed my help. I have heard, from the jungle grapevine, that you have your eyes on this village. Beware! You will have to first fight me before you can lay a hand on even one villager's hair!'

Abhishek the lion backed into his hut in fright. A monster as guardian! Why, he had never heard of this. Just then the pretend-monster took a step forward and lurched towards him. Bela's uncle let out his finest, loudest roar. That was enough! The lion impostor took to his heels and fled into the forest. He ran and ran till he reached his den. Life in the jungle was so much safer than the village, he thought, panting. Never again would he even dare to step that way!

Meanwhile, in the village, Bela, her father and her uncle threw off the blankets and sticks and did a dance of joy. The next morning everyone wondered what had happened to Abhishek and came to console Bela because they thought her fiancé had run away. Bela listened to all of them and smiled secretly to herself. She had got the better of that cunning lion!

The Magic Jug

Vidur was a good-natured man. Even though he was poor, he was always ready to help people in need. Vidur's neighbour, Vineet, was rich. But he was a mean and jealous man.

One night, a stranger knocked on Vineet's door. It was past midnight and Vineet was annoyed at being woken up from his sleep. 'What do you want?' he asked the stranger rudely. The man explained that he was a traveller, hungry and lost, looking for food and shelter for the night. 'I never help lazy, unknown people,' barked Vineet and banged the door shut.

The stranger walked to Vidur's house and asked for food and shelter. Kind-hearted Vidur welcomed him into his humble one-room house and warmed up the leftovers of his dinner for the man. Then he insisted the stranger sleep in his bed while he slept on a mattress on the floor.

The next morning when he woke up, he found the stranger was about to leave. Before going on his way, the stranger rummaged in his large bag and took out an ordinary piece of cloth and a plain, earthen jug.

He handed these to Vidur and said, 'You shared your small meal and gave me your bed for the night. I will always be grateful. Here are two things that will be of use to you when you are in need. But remember, you must use them only when you need them the most, and take just enough to meet your requirements. Don't try to get rich using these.'

With these words, the stranger left. Vidur looked at the cloth and jug carefully, then laughed loudly to himself. Perhaps the stranger had been a bit crazy—how could these old articles be of help? He tucked them away in a corner of his cupboard and soon forgot about them.

That year was difficult and Vidur was not able to make ends meet. His little farm had not produced enough harvest. He decided to go to the market in the city and look for some work. It was a very hot day. When Vidur was about to leave, he saw the sun high up in the sky, and so he decided to carry a cloth to cover his head. Suddenly, he remembered the strange visitor's gift. He hunted for the cloth and found it tucked away in the back of his cupboard. It had become dusty and musty. Vidur shook it vigorously to clean the dust and, to his astonishment, a gold coin dropped out!

Vidur picked up the coin and wondered how it got into the cloth. Perhaps the stranger had hidden it there?

He shook the cloth to see if any more coins would fall out, but none appeared. Well, he could hardly get rich with one coin, though it would help him tide over his current condition. He used it to buy the things he needed, and gave the small change that was left to a beggar.

Vidur soon realized that the cloth produced money only when he was in desperate need and the money was just enough to fulfil his requirements. With the money, he put his farm in order and became richer. He also never forgot to help those less fortunate than him. This made him a very popular person.

Vidur's prosperity had not gone unnoticed by the jealous Vineet. He started spying on his neighbour to see where he got his money from, and one day, peeping in through the window, he saw Vidur shaking the old piece of cloth and picking up the coins that fell out. He also noticed a large earthen jug standing next to the cloth in the cupboard. 'The foolish, foolish man!' he thought to himself. 'If that tattered old cloth can give him one coin each time, think how many that massive jug will produce. Just like goody-goody Vidur not to see what the jug can give him!' And it was true. Vidur had always been satisfied with whatever he got from the cloth and had not thought of finding out what the jug might produce.

As soon as Vidur left the house, Vineet went inside, picked up the jug and sprinted back home. Eagerly, he turned the jug upside down. Out rolled an apple. It had an unusual purple-red colour. Vineet had never seen anything like this. It was irresistible! He picked it up and bit into the apple, crunching quickly, thinking all the while that gold would soon begin showering down. But wait a minute! What was this happening to him? His ears were getting bigger, his arms and legs were becoming longer, with what looked like hoofs at the end, and was that a tail he could feel growing behind him? Vineet rushed to the mirror, and when he saw himself, started braying in terror. He had turned into a donkey!

Vidur heard the loud braying coming from his neighbour's house and rushed to see what the matter

was. When he found a sad-looking donkey in the house with his old earthen jug next to it, he understood what Vineet had tried to do. He picked up the jug and shook it this way and that, hoping somehow to turn the donkey-Vineet back to his old human form. But nothing happened. The jug was empty and Vineet would have to remain a donkey. Vidur took pity on the donkey and took him home, where he looked after him, giving him food and comforting him whenever he shed tears into the hay.

And then one day, walking down the road, lo and behold, whom should he see but the same stranger who had given him the cloth and jug. A delighted Vidur pounced on him and dragged him home.

'You must transform my friend back into a human being!' he begged.

The donkey brayed softly and apologetically. The man thought for a while. Then he said, 'I can turn him back into a man. But you will have to give up the magic cloth.'

'I agree!' Vidur agreed without a moment's hesitation. 'I was never rich, and I am used to working hard. I will find a way to make my living, but it breaks my heart to see Vineet like this.'

The stranger smiled. Then he muttered something into the jug, picked up the cloth and went away. No sooner had he turned the corner than Vineet turned back into a man again.

The two hugged each other. Vineet thanked his friend profusely. From that day on, they helped each other in whatever ways they could and neither was unhappy again.

The Wishing Tree

Ram and Lakshman were brothers. They lived with their mother, Geeta, in a little village by a river. They did not have a father, and Geeta had brought up both the boys. But Ram was her stepson, and she treated him very badly. She would not give him enough food to eat, or new clothes, and made him do all the work around the house. She showered all her affection on Lakshman, who was her own son, and looked after him well. In spite of this, the two boys were very fond of each other and Ram, the elder one, always watched out for his younger brother, Lakshman.

Sometimes, when Geeta was in a particularly bad temper, she would set Ram all kinds of impossible tasks to finish. One day she told him, 'I am going to the market. I want you to fill this drum with water from the river. Mind you, the work should be completed by the time I return in the evening. Here, take this bucket to carry water from the river.' So saying, she handed him the smallest, oldest bucket they had.

Ram looked at the drum. It was huge. The river was some distance away from their little house. Clearly, it would take him the whole day to fill it using the ancient bucket. Without wasting any time, he took the bucket to the river and filled it to the brim. But by the time he reached the drum, there was hardly any water left! When Ram examined the bucket closely, he found a little hole at the bottom. He realized he would never be able to fill the drum with this bucket.

Just then, Lakshman came up. 'What is it, brother?' he asked. 'Why do you look so worried?' When Ram explained his problem, Lakshman immediately offered to help. 'I will put my little finger in the hole to stop it,' he suggested. 'Then the water will not leak.'

In this way, the two brothers worked together and completed the task. In the evening, Geeta returned from the market, ready to scold Ram for not completing his work, but to her amazement she saw the drum right by the doorstep, filled to the brim. She understood that Lakshman must have helped Ram. She was very angry.

Next day, she called Ram and said, 'Bring a cartload of wood from the forest.' Again, with Lakshman's help, Ram completed the work.

The day after that Geeta said, 'I want you to cross the river and go to the green meadow on the other bank. The grass there is tall and green. Bring many bundles of grass for our sheep. The rest I will sell in the market.' Then she looked at Lakshman and said, 'You will come with me to the market today to help me carry my things.'

Lakshman had no choice but to go with his mother. Ram, too, set off. When he reached the river bank, he looked across to the other side. Sure enough, he could see the tall and fresh grass that grew in that green meadow. He wondered why no one grazed animals in the meadow.

An old shepherd passed by. 'Hello, uncle,' Ram hailed him.

The shepherd nodded. 'What are you doing by the river?' he asked.

'I'm going to cross the river and go to that meadow,' Ram explained. 'But tell me, why does no one use the meadow to graze cattle?'

The old shepherd looked at Ram as though he were mad. 'Are you a fool, young boy?' he growled. 'To get grass from that meadow you will have to risk your life. Don't you know the dangers of cutting grass there?'

When Ram shook his head, the shepherd explained, 'That meadow is home to a large pack of fierce wolves. Anyone who enters the meadow will be eaten by them. Not even a bone will be left for others to know what happened.'

Ram stared at him in dismay. 'My mother has asked me to bring grass from there. I have to go!' he said quietly. The old man looked into his determined eyes and sighed. 'Then I will tell you a secret that my grandfather told me. It's the secret of how to come out of the meadow alive. When I was a young boy like you, I used to go there using this secret. Now I am too old. But you look like a determined fellow, and if I don't tell you the secret, you will surely die.' The shepherd paused for breath. Then he continued, 'When you reach the meadow, the wolves will surround you. If you are good at heart, the wolves will leave you alone. When you finish your work and are ready to come back, the wolves will come to get you again. At that time you must roar ferociously, like a lion. The wolves will run away and not harm you.'

Ram thanked the old man profusely for telling him this secret and set off across the river. As soon as he set foot in the meadow, a snarling, salivating pack of wolves surrounded him. Ram dropped down on his knees and prayed hard, 'If I am doing the right thing and am good at heart, please save me.' Immediately the wolves ran away. Ram cut a lot of grass and tied it into bundles. Then he sat down under the shade of an apple tree to rest for a while.

As he lay down and looked up at the tree, he saw three golden apples hanging from the branches. His stomach growling loudly in hunger, he quickly climbed the tree and picked one apple. Holding the apple in his hand, he bit into it and thought, 'I wish my mother gave me nice things to eat, so I would not always be so hungry.' No sooner had he thought this than he realized that his stomach was full—his hunger had disappeared.

Ram wondered if these were magic apples which fulfilled wishes. So he said, as he picked another apple and bit into it, 'I wish I could be strong and healthy, with some nice clothes which are not torn and dirty.' And sure enough, he felt himself growing taller and stronger! His raggedy clothes fell off his back and he found himself wearing clean, new clothes. Delighted, Ram kissed the tree. Then, since this was all he wanted, he got down, thanked the tree again and went back towards the river, swinging the bundles of grass in his muscular arms. When the wolves came for him, he made the noise of an angry lion and they disappeared in the blink of an eye!

When Geeta saw her stepson return from the dreaded meadow looking stronger and healthier than ever, clad in nice, new clothes, she was horrified. How could this be? Ram, who was simple and honest, told his stepmother and brother all about the wish-giving apples on the tree. Geeta was green with jealousy. To think her good-for-nothing stepson had got all those wishes and her own darling Lakshman nothing! She hatched a plan.

The next day she told Ram, 'You help me carry all those bundles of grass to the market.' Then she took Lakshman aside and whispered to him, 'Go to the meadow and pick the wish-giving apple. Ask for lots of money to make us rich beyond our imagination.'

Then Geeta set off for the market with Ram, and Lakshman made his way to the meadow. When Ram returned home in the afternoon, he looked around for his brother. 'Where is he?' he asked their mother.

'He has gone to the magic tree to pick an apple and wish for lots of wealth for us,' Geeta replied. Ram looked at

her in horror. 'But I did not tell him the secret about the wolves!' he cried. 'They will tear him to pieces!' Without waiting a second longer, he raced down to the river. Geeta ran after him. By the time she reached the river, Ram was already halfway across. She could only sit and cry and pray.

When Ram reached the meadow, the wolves were nowhere to be seen. He spotted them gathered below the apple tree. He ran there. Lakshman had somehow managed to climb the tree. Now he was trapped there, the wolves waiting for him to come down so they could tear him apart. Ram roared like a lion and the wolves vanished. Then, he climbed the tree and reached his frightened, sobbing brother. Lakshman was holding the third apple in his hand and muttering something. Putting his arm around his brother, Ram asked, 'Why didn't you use the last apple to come home safely?'

Lakshman wiped his nose and said, 'I know my mother loves me more than she loves you. So I wished that she should love you more than me. That is more important to me than returning home safely. If something were to happen to me, she would have one son to love and cherish.' Ram's eyes filled with tears. He hugged his brother. 'Let's go home,' he whispered. 'Our mother is waiting for us.'

The boys quickly got down and crossed the river. They found their mother sitting there, waiting anxiously. As she gathered her son into her arms, Ram told her about the wolves and Lakshman's wish. Pulling him into her embrace too, Geeta learnt a lesson from her two young children—to love without looking for a reason. And though they never knew whether it was because of the wishing apple or if their mother had changed after seeing their love for each other, Ram and Lakshman lived happily together, sharing Geeta's love.

Tit for Tat

Kiran and Varun were good friends, even though Kiran was cunning and Varun was a simple person. Once, when they were travelling together, it started raining very hard. The two had to stop and take shelter. Standing under a huge banyan tree, they huddled close to the trunk, shivering. There, in a little hollow, they found a pot with a tight lid. They managed to prise open the lid and found to their delight that the pot was full of gold! The two friends decided to divide the money when they reached home. But by now it was dark and they could not see anything. They had to spend the night under the tree.

In the middle of the night, while Varun slept soundly, Kiran woke up, removed all the gold from the pot and filled it with stones. Shutting the lid tightly again, he went back to sleep. The next morning they went back home, carefully carrying the pot. When they opened it, they found only stones. Varun was heartbroken. 'Whatever could have happened to all that gold?' he wailed. Kiran pretended to console him. 'Perhaps it was a magic pot, and the gold was never meant for us. Let's throw it away before it does us any harm.' He took the pot from Varun's hands and threw it as far as possible.

Poor Varun at first believed his friend's story. But after a few days, he noticed that Kiran had suddenly become very rich. He was spending money like water, buying whatever he laid his eyes on. Now Varun understood what must have happened to all that gold in the pot. Furious at being made a fool of by his friend, he hatched a plan to get even.

He went to the town artist and asked him to make a clay image of Kiran. Then he purchased two monkeys and brought them home. Every day he trained the monkeys to eat their meals sitting in the lap of the clay image. After many weeks, the monkeys would eat only when they were seated in the statue's lap.

Varun then put the next part of his plan into action. He invited Kiran's son and daughter home for a meal. Since they were very fond of their Uncle Varun, they happily agreed.

Varun whispered his plan to them and the children laughed, agreeing to do as he said. What an adventure, they thought.

When his children did not return home by evening, Kiran got worried and went to Varun's house to look for them. Varun invited him in, offered a seat and brought some tea. 'Forget the tea, Varun,' Kiran bellowed. 'Tell me where my kids are!'

Varun had hidden the children in another room. 'Here they are,' he announced, and brought out his two pet monkeys. As soon as the monkeys saw Kiran, they thought he was the statue in whose lap they sat every day to eat their meals. They jumped on to his lap and started looking for food in his pockets. Kiran was very angry. 'Call these monkeys away from me! Tell me where my children are, before I call in the king's soldiers!'

Varun pretended to be surprised. 'My friend! Can you not recognize your own children sitting on your lap?'

'How dare you say these monkeys are my dear children!' shouted Kiran, pushing the monkeys away, nearly bursting with rage.

'Don't be angry, Kiran,' Varun replied. 'As soon as I fed your children their lunch, they turned into monkeys.'

'You expect me to believe such a story? How can children become monkeys?'

Varun smiled. 'In the same way gold can turn into stone, my friend,' he answered quietly.

Now Kiran understood what Varun was trying to tell him. He turned red with shame. He promised to share half of his newly gained wealth with Varun and went home with his children. And whenever he saw a monkey after that, he remembered his cheating ways and never tried to trick anyone again.

Sow a Witch

Veeru was an adventurous, bright boy. His teacher, Dharmendra, was very fond of him.

When Veeru completed his studies, he told his teacher, 'Guruji, you have given me so much knowledge. Is there anything I can do for you in return?'

His teacher smiled and replied, 'I taught you because it was my duty, not for any reward. But there is something that I have always wanted, and I think only you can get it for me. Legend has it that the gods created a Book of Knowledge, into which they poured their divine learning. But it got into the hands of a witch, who has kept the book with her ever since. People say she lives high up in the remotest corner of the Himalayas. Only the bravest and strongest of men can hope to get there and retrieve that book. I think you are such a person. If you do get this book, you will do all of mankind the greatest service.'

Veeru was charged up with enthusiasm when he heard this story. 'I will go there and get the book!' he declared.

'Then keep these three pebbles,' his teacher said. 'Use them only when you don't know what else to do.'

Veeru set off with the three pebbles in his pocket. After a long and difficult journey of many days, he reached the witch's lair. The witch was fast asleep inside her cottage. Veeru spotted the book lying on a table near her bed. It was a large, heavy book and he realized it would not be easy to run away with it. So he threw a pebble at the book and said, 'Make the book small.' Immediately, the book became the size of a small piece of paper. Veeru tiptoed into the room and picked it up. No sooner had he slipped it into his pocket than the witch woke up. She grabbed him and said, 'Ah ha! a human . . . Yummm . . . I've not eaten tender man-meat for a long time! Come, my little raisin, let me eat you in a gulp!'

Veeru was not scared. He smiled politely and said, 'Sure. But let me go

to the lake and freshen up. I am dirty after my long journey.'

The witch agreed. She tied a rope around his waist and let him go out to the lake to clean up. Veeru untied the rope, slipped it around a tree trunk, placed the second pebble near the tree and whispered to it, 'Talk like me.' Then he quietly ran off from there.

The witch waited for some time for Veeru to come back. When there was no sign of him, she jerked the rope and shouted, 'Are you there?'

The pebble replied in Veeru's voice, 'Yes, I am here.'

After some time the witch shouted out to Veeru again, and once more the pebble replied in his voice. This happened a few more times, but the witch was getting very angry. Finally, she gave the rope a hard pull. The tree came flying out, uprooted. She understood that she had been tricked and went after Veeru at great speed.

But Veeru had got a good start. He threw the third pebble and made it create mountains, rivers, volcanoes and other obstacles for the witch. When he reached his teacher, he handed the book to him and begged to be hidden somewhere. Quickly, his teacher found a hiding

place for him. Then he calmly went about cooking a meal.

Some days later, the witch arrived huffing and puffing. 'Where is that boy?' she shrieked. 'I know he is hiding here. I can smell him! Hand him to me.'

'Certainly,' replied Dharmendra, 'but first eat something. You must be hungry.' And he served the witch a simple meal of chapattis and vegetables. The witch gobbled down this strange food. When she finished and had burped happily, she began to feel sleepy. Then Dharmendra said, 'How could Veeru escape from someone as strong and clever as you? Perhaps your strength is just a myth. I don't believe it!'

The witch chuckled. 'You want me to show you how strong I am? Come on, test me.'

Dharmendra quickly said, 'Become as big as a mountain and touch the sky.'

The witch swelled up and touched the sky.

'Now become as small as a seed,' Dharmendra challenged.

Without thinking, the witch turned herself into a tiny seed. Quick as a flash, Dharmendra picked her up and sowed her deep into the earth, where she lay trapped forever. The plant that grew out of the witch-seed was a soya bean plant. Soya bean contains a lot of strength. So eating soya bean will make you as strong as the witch!

Read More in Puffin

Grandma's Bag of Stories
Sudha Murty

When Grandma opens her bag of stories, everyone gathers around.

Who can resist a good story, especially when it's being told by Grandma? From her bag emerge tales of kings and cheats, monkeys and mice, bears and gods. Here comes the bear who ate some really bad dessert and got very angry; a lazy man who would not put out a fire till it reached his beard; a princess who got turned into an onion; a queen who discovered silk, and many more weird and wonderful people and animals.

Grandma tells the stories over long summer days and nights, as seven children enjoy life in her little town. The stories entertain, educate and provide hours of enjoyment to them. So come, why don't you too join in the fun?

Read More in Puffin

How I Taught My Grandmother to Read and Other Stories
Sudha Murty

What do you do when your grandmother asks you to teach her the alphabet? Or the President of India takes you on a train ride with him? Or a teacher gives you more marks than you deserve?

These are just some of the questions you will find answered in this delightful collection of stories recounting real-life incidents from the life of Sudha Murty, teacher, social worker and bestselling writer. There is the engaging story about one of her students who frequently played truant from school, the account of how her mother's advice to save money came in handy when she wanted to help her husband start a software company and the heart-warming tale of the promise she made—and fulfilled—to her grandfather, to ensure that her little village library would always be well-supplied with books.

Funny, spirited and inspiring, each of these stories teaches a valuable lesson about the importance of doing what you believe is right and having the courage to realize your dreams.

Read More in Puffin

The Magic Drum and Other Favourite Stories
Sudha Murty

A princess who thinks she was a bird, a coconut that cost a thousand rupees, and a shepherd with a bag of words . . .

Kings and misers, princes and paupers, wise men and foolish boys, the funniest and oddest men and women come alive in this sparkling new collection of stories. The clever princess will only marry the man who can ask her a question she cannot answer; the orphan boy outwits his greedy uncles with a bag of ash; and an old couple in distress is saved by a magic drum.

Sudha Murty's grandparents told her some of these stories when she was a child; others she heard from her friends from around the world. These delightful and timeless folktales have been her favourites for years, and she has recounted them many times over to the young people in her life. With this collection, they will be enjoyed by many more readers, of all ages.

Read More in Puffin

The Magic of the Lost Temple
Sudha Murty

A new novel by India's favourite storyteller

City girl Nooni is surprised at the pace of life in her grandparents' village in Karnataka. But she quickly gets used to the gentle routine there and involves herself in a flurry of activities, including papad making, organizing picnics and learning to ride a cycle, with her new-found friends.

Things get exciting when Nooni stumbles upon an ancient, fabled stepwell right in the middle of a forest near the village.

Join the intrepid Nooni on the adventure of a lifetime in this much-awaited book by Sudha Murty that is heart-warming, charming and absolutely unputdownable.